RUPERT, POLLY, AND DAISY

To librarians, parents, and teachers:

Rupert, Polly, and Daisy is a Parents Magazine READ ALOUD Original — one title in a series of colorfully illustrated and fun-to-read stories that young readers will be sure to come back to time and time again.

Now, in this special school and library edition of *Rupert, Polly, and Daisy*, adults have an even greater opportunity to increase children's responsiveness to reading and learning — and to have fun every step of the way.

When you finish this story, check the special section at the back of the book. There you will find games, projects, things to talk about, and other educational activities designed to make reading enjoyable by giving children and adults a chance to play together, work together, and talk over the story they have just read.

For a free color catalog describing Gareth Stevens' list of high-quality books, call 1-800-542-2595 (USA) or 1-800-461-9120 (Canada). Gareth Stevens' Fax: (414) 225-0377.

Parents Magazine READ ALOUD Originals:

A Garden for Miss Mouse
Aren't You Forgetting Something, Fiona?
Bicycle Bear
The Biggest Shadow in the Zoo
Bread and Honey
Buggly Bear's Hiccup Cure
But No Elephants
Cats! Cats! Cats!
The Clown-Arounds
The Clown-Arounds Go on Vacation
Elephant Goes to School
The Fox with Cold Feet
Get Well, Clown-Arounds!
The Ghost in Dobbs Diner
The Giggle Book
The Goat Parade
Golly Gump Swallowed a Fly
Henry Babysits

Henry Goes West
Henry's Awful Mistake
Henry's Important Date
The Housekeeper's Dog
The Little Witch Sisters
The Man Who Cooked for Himself
Milk and Cookies
Miss Mopp's Lucky Day
No Carrots for Harry!
Oh, So Silly!
The Old Man and the Afternoon Cat
One Little Monkey
The Peace-and-Quiet Diner
Pets I Wouldn't Pick
Pickle Things
Pigs in the House
Rabbit's New Rug
Rupert, Polly, and Daisy
Sand Cake

Septimus Bean and His Amazing Machine
Sheldon's Lunch
Sherlock Chick and the Giant Egg Mystery
Sherlock Chick's First Case
The Silly Tail Book
Snow Lion
Socks for Supper
Sweet Dreams, Clown-Arounds!
Ten Furry Monsters
There's No Place Like Home
This Farm is a Mess
Those Terrible Toy-Breakers
Up Goes Mr. Downs
The Very Bumpy Bus Ride
Where's Rufus?
Who Put the Pepper in the Pot?
Witches Four

Library of Congress Cataloging-in-Publication Data

Silver, Jody.
    Rupert, Polly, and Daisy/ by Jody Silver.
        p.   cm. -- (Parents magazine read aloud original)
    "North American library edition"--T.p. verso.
    Summary: When Rupert seems to be paying more attention to Daisy the new fish, Polly, the bird, decides to fly away.
    ISBN 0-8368-0994-7
    [1. Birds--Fiction. 2. Fishes--Fiction. 3. Pets--Fiction. 4. Friendship--Fiction.] I. Title. II. Series.
PZ7.S5857Ru 1994
[E]--dc20   94-16227

This North American library edition published in 1994 by Gareth Stevens Publishing, 1555 North RiverCenter Drive, Suite 201, Milwaukee, Wisconsin, 53212, USA, under an arrangement with Pages, Inc., St. Petersburg, Florida.

Printed in the United States of America

1 2 3 4 5 6 7 8 9 99 98 97 96 95 94

Rupert, Polly, and Daisy

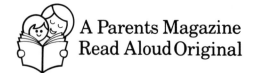

A Parents Magazine
Read Aloud Original

Rupert, Polly, and Daisy
by Jody Silver

Parents Magazine Press • New York
Gareth Stevens Publishing • Milwaukee

To Stephanie C.
and my sister, Sue

It was quite a day when Daisy
came to live with Rupert and Polly.
They fixed up a cozy spot for her
and watched as she swam about.

Rupert read to Polly
and to Daisy, too.

They sang
Polly's song.

Then they sang
Daisy's song.

11

When Daisy heard her song,
she started to dance!

Rupert was amazed and called
the neighbors in to watch.

As soon as Rupert realized
how clever Daisy was,
he taught her many things.

Then one day Rupert built Daisy
a castle to play in.
For the tower, he borrowed
Polly's bell.
Polly didn't like that at all.

Rupert tried to make
Polly feel better
by singing her a song.

*Shoo fly,
don't bother me!
Shoo fly,
don't bother me!*

Suddenly, Daisy started
to play along!

Once again, Rupert ran
to get the neighbors.

This was more than Polly could stand.
Even though she knew Rupert would roar,
Polly reached into the fish bowl
to take back her bell.

But Daisy was not about to give up
the only sound she had ever made.
When Polly started to pull the bell up,
Daisy grabbed the string.

21

Polly knew Rupert would never forgive
her if anything happened to Daisy.

So she had to put back the bell.

When Rupert returned with the neighbors
he began to sing as Daisy played along.

*For I belong
to somebody!*

Meantime, Polly packed her things.

Just as Polly flew toward the window,
Daisy splashed Rupert.
Rupert turned his head in time
to see Polly fly away.

Rupert and the neighbors
ran after Polly.
But she was too fast and they
lost her at Town Square.

Then Rupert saw something he
hoped would bring Polly back.

He ran into Town Hall and
up to the bell tower.

Loudly, he rang out Polly's song.
All over town they heard it.

Polly heard it too
and flew into sight.

Polly flew near Rupert,
but she still was not sure
she wanted to go home.

As she backed farther
and farther away,
she could see that Rupert was
holding on by only a thin rope.

So Polly flew to Rupert.
Down below they cheered.

Then they sang Polly's song
while Rupert played along.

And together they went home.

As soon as Daisy saw Polly,
she flipped right up from her bowl.

Daisy was happy to see Polly.
And Polly was glad to see Daisy, too.

Rupert promised not to take any
of Polly's toys without asking first.

Then Rupert, Polly, and Daisy
danced and sang until it was time for bed.

Notes to Grown-ups

Major Themes

Here is a quick guide to the significant themes and concepts at work in *Rupert, Polly, and Daisy*:

- Sharing with a friend or a new baby – as Polly learned to do.
- Respect for another's property – something Rupert had forgotten about.

Step-by-step Ideas for Reading and Talking

Here are some ideas for further give-and-take between grown-ups and children. The following topics encourage creative discussion of *Rupert, Polly, and Daisy* and invite the kind of open-ended response that is consistent with many contemporary approaches to reading, including Whole Language:

- Daisy could benefit from having Polly's bell. But when Rupert took it without asking, Polly felt unwanted, as if she had been replaced by the new fish. If you have more than one child, this might be a familiar problem.
- How did Polly show her concern for Rupert? What might have happened if Rupert had continued to hang onto the thin rope?
- How did Daisy show her concern for Polly? Would Polly have come back if Rupert hadn't gone after her? Would Rupert have known Polly was leaving if Daisy hadn't splashed him? Children love "what if. . ." questions, and a series like this can be good training in logical thinking.

Games for Learning

Games and activities can stimulate young readers and listeners alike to find out more about words, numbers, and ideas. Here are more ideas for turning learning into fun:

Pet Store Math

A visit to a pet store can provide opportunities for your child to classify, count, compare, and strengthen other basic math and science skills. Look for the biggest pet and the smallest pet; count the number of various animals.

Ask your child which toys she or he thinks a particular pet would like most. Which toys does your child think Polly and Daisy would prefer?

Goldfish Math

You can use goldfish crackers (available in most supermarkets or food stores) to help your child review math skills like classifying, counting, or basic graphing. Purchase several types of goldfish crackers and put a mix of about twenty crackers into a container. Ask your child to sort the crackers into the various types, and then to count the number of crackers in each set. Your child could then make a simple bar or pictorial graph (using stickers or simple illustrations) to illustrate the numbers.

About the Author/Artist

JODY SILVER has written and illustrated several books for children, including an earlier story about Rupert and Polly. This book is based on her feelings about having a new baby sister in her family when she was growing up. She says, "At first, I wasn't sure I liked the idea of sharing things with my sister, but now we get along well. In fact, I've dedicated this book to her." Jody Silver lives in New York City with her husband and daughter.